The Lighthouse Keeper's Daughter

A Play in One Act

Muriel and Richard Eldridge

A SAMUEL FRENCH ACTING EDITION

FOUNDED 1830

SAMUELFRENCH.COM
SAMUELFRENCH-LONDON.CO.UK

FOR PRODUCTION ENQUIRIES

UNITED STATES AND CANADA

Info@SamuelFrench.com

1-866-598-8449

UNITED KINGDOM AND EUROPE

Plays@SamuelFrench-London.co.uk

020-7255-4302

Each title is subject to availability from Samuel French, depending upon country of performance. Please be aware that *THE LIGHTHOUSE KEEPER'S DAUGHTER* may not be licensed by Samuel French in your territory. Professional and amateur producers should contact the nearest Samuel French office or licensing partner to verify availability.

DESCRIPTION OF CHARACTERS

THE LIGHTHOUSE KEEPER: *A man of 50 or so, tanned face, rugged build, clad in oilskins and rubber boots.*

HIS WIFE: *A buxom, red-cheeked woman, wearing a big kitchen-apron; none of your frilly bride's equipment, but a goodly-sized generous cover-all; hair screwed into a knot; glasses.*

HIS DAUGHTER: *A fair young thing of about 16 with braids dangling below her sun-bonnet; short gingham dress, socks, slippers.*

VILLAIN: *Nondescript in age and build; a black-browed, black-hearted skulker, his cap pulled furtively over his eyes; wearing either an old sweater with neckerchief or a loud suit.*

DOCTOR: *A clean-cut, attractive young hero in a natty business suit and fedora, or trim overcoat and derby. He is alert and observant.*

The Lighthouse Keeper's Daughter

SET: *No definite stage set needed, nor special entrances. May be played anywhere that affords a single entrance, Right, Left or Centre. Only furniture needed is a pseudo-lighthouse, which may be anything from an ash-stand, pedestal type bearing a candle-stick, to a bridge-lamp. A small table will be found handy to hold the* WIFE's *chowder bowl, but is not essential*

LIGHTING: *No special equipment. Would suggest center-spot or side floods.*

The action is entirely pantomime as the text is read, faithfully following every suggested movement, almost word by word. If done with an air of utmost seriousness, the facial expression carrying out the "drama," the humorous effect will be greatly heightened.

Each time a character climbs the stair to the tower he should circle about the "lighthouse" at least four or five times with exaggerated pretense at stair-climbing, lifting the feet twelve inches or so from the floor at every step. Remember to reverse direction when descending the stairs. When more than one character is going up or down, allow sufficient distance between to simulate the real condition.

The final tableau shows the lovers with clasped hands, kneeling before the parents, who assume an attitude of benediction as the Curtain falls. If no curtain is used, the cast may leave the stage two by two in solemn parade, with suitable demeanor.

PROLOGUE

Upon a lonely island, amid the rolling wave,
There stands a lonely lighthouse whose base the salt
    seas lave.
A strong and stalwart keeper with wife and daughter
    fair
Resided in that lighthouse and kept it shining there.

DRAMA

One sunset as the maiden gazed sadly out to sea,
"Alas!" she thought, "How empty all life appears to
    me.
Now can it be Adventure will wholly pass me by?
So far from all excitement must I both live and die?"
Ah, little knew that maiden if truth or not she spoke,
Or that, when least expected, Life has its little joke.

That night her doughty father climbed up the narrow
    stair
And lit, as was his custom, the lamp that waited there.
His duty once accomplished, he leaned against the
    door
And reaching in his pocket took out the meagre store
Of pay received that morning and covering all the
    year.
'Twas not a mighty fortune and yet he held it dear.
He proudly turned it over to let the lamp-light shine
On every coin he counted—to him a golden mine.

Below him in the shadows there skulked a villain
     grim;
He knew the keeper's habits and envious was of him.
He'd loved the keeper's daughter, he coveted his gold,
And in his heart he plotted on both revenge untold.
He tiptoed past the kitchen to where the stairs began,
Then stealthily he climbed them to seek the hapless
     man.
As round and round he mounted, his greed was
     mounting, too.
At last he reached his victim and cruelly he slew.
Forthwith he snatched his dagger and wiped it on his
     pants,—
He never gave the keeper a single backward glance,
But grabbed the bag of moneys and started down the
     stair
Nor stopped one breathless moment until he gained
     the air.

The keeper's wife had ready a chowder good and hot
And she began to worry when he descended not.
She said unto her daughter, "Just leave the light
     turned low
And I will climb the staircase to see what keeps him
     so."
She toiled about the tower with slow and steady pace
Not recking of the sorrow that soon would blanch her
     face.
Around and round she mounted with quick and
     labored breath
While on the stairs above her lay a grim and ghastly
     death.

A cry rang on the darkness, a shriek to freeze the
     blood
As the keeper's lowly helpmate bewailed her widow-
     hood.

With hand that shook with horror she touched his
    clammy brow,
Then stumbled *down* the stairway—reached ground
    she knew not how.
"Your Dad," she gasped, "your father—" Alarmed
    said daughter then,
"Why, Mama, what's the trouble? Oh, speak to me
    again."
In spite of tears and sobbings they struggled to the
    top,
Around and round and round again as if they could
    not stop.

"Oh, daughter, fetch a doctor," the stricken mother
    cried.
Without a word, by terror spurred, the daughter duly
    hied.
She seized a boat, she seized the oars, she seized the
    anchor, too,
And through the night, urged on by fright, that little
    rowboat flew.
"Oh, Doctor, Doctor, Doctor," she sobbed with every
    breath,
"If it be fate, come not too late, but save my Pa from
    death."

And now she's found the doctor, again the oar-locks
    click.
Against the foam, she rows him home. Thinks he,
    "This girl is slick."
They pass the dashing currents, they pass the rugged
    rock,
With might and main, despite the strain, they reach
    the lighthouse dock.
Then upward, ever upward, a breathless couple toiled
To where the wounded keeper with blood the floor-
    boards soiled.

And downward, ever downward, they bore the sorry
    load;
Into the cozy kitchen with gasping breath they strode.
The doctor did his noblest with every tool he had
And soon a rising color renewed what hope they had.
The keeper oped his eyelids, he drew a deeper breath,
The workers felt assurance that they had cheated
    death.

EPILOGUE

The sequel of this story is evident and clear—
The doctor and the daughter, their troth they plighted
    dear.
The keeper gave his blessing; the wife, she gave hers,
    too.
Adventure, Love and Honor—each one received its
    due.

THE LIGHTHOUSE KEEPER'S DAUGHTER

PROPERTIES

1. The Lighthouse may be any tall thin piece of furniture. A piano lamp or an ash-stand serves excellently.
2. Bag of money—metal washers in a salt or sugar bag clink well.
3. Dagger—an obvious paper cutter or ice-pick.
4. Chowder-pot—any good-sized kettle set on a kitchen chair.
5. Row-boat and oars—use ironing board laid flat on the floor for boat, and cane and unbrella or golf sticks for oars; improvised anchor and rope.
6. Doctor's kit—traveling bag or suitcase containing carpentering tools—hammer, saw, pliers, screw-driver, etc.

COSTUMES

Lighthouse Keeper: Oilskins and rain hat.

Keeper's Wife: Large apron, spectacles, may wear dusting cap.

Keeper's Daughter: Sun-bonnet, hair in braids or curls, simple dress, gingham or print. Flat-heeled shoes and socks.

Doctor: Derby hat or Fedora, business suit, gloves.

Villain: Soft hat or cap pulled low over eyes, overcoat with collar turned up or handkerchief about neck. May wear mask. Slinking furtive air.

Reader should be inconspicuously dressed so as not to distract attention from the play.